This Walker book

belongs to:

____

____

For my god-daughter, Katie A. M.

For my sister, Jo S. R.

First published 2015 by Walker Books Ltd, 87 Vauxhall Walk,
London SE11 5HJ

This edition published 2016

10 9 8 7 6 5 4 3 2 1

This book has been typeset in Clarendon T Light

Printed and bound in Malaysia

British Library Cataloguing in Publication Data: a catalogue record for this book is available from the British Library.

ISBN 978-1-4063-6591-7

www.walker.co.uk

The author would like to thank Rael Meyerowitz and Jo Gaskell for their support and advice.

A BOOK of feelings

starring
SAM, KATE
and
FUZZY BEAN

Amanda McCardie

illustrated by
Salvatore Rubbino

WALKER BOOKS
AND SUBSIDIARIES
LONDON • BOSTON • SYDNEY • AUCKLAND

Sam and Kate live with their mum and dad
and Fuzzy Bean, their dog.
This book is about their feelings and
it starts with feeling **happy**!

So many things make Sam and Kate feel happy.

A cuddle, a story, a game in the park ... drawing a picture, catching a ball...

and most of all,
deep down,
knowing
they're **loved**.

Even when Mum's in a hurry or Dad gets **cross**, they know they're loved.

A happy Sam might share his toys.

A happy Kate might hug the dog.

They want to say “Thank you” and “Sorry” more.

But Sam and Kate are not always happy both at once
and they don't feel happy all the time.

Quite often, for instance, they feel **grumpy**.

When Kate feels this way, she can't say thank you OR sorry.

Nor can Sam!

He doesn't feel **loving** or kind at all.

Sometimes, Sam feels **embarrassed**. When he tripped over the football in the middle of a match, he felt so foolish he almost cried.

Kate feels **shy** with children she doesn't know.
She looks at the ground and can't speak,
then her voice comes out in a whisper.

Reading out loud makes Sam **nervous**.
He gets a sick feeling, as if
he's in a lift going down too fast.

Some nights Kate feels **frightened** of the dark. She feels shivery and clammy and her heart thumps too hard until Dad comes to switch on the light.

Sam gets scared of monsters (though he doesn't mind feeling a little bit scared).

And Fuzzy Bean is terrified of thunderstorms.

Don't worry,
Fuzzy.
I'm here.

There are also times when Sam and Kate feel **sad**.

Sam cried when Guinea the guinea-pig died.

So did Dad.

Fuzzy quite often wanted to eat Guinea
but he still came to the funeral.

Kate felt sad when she said goodbye to her teacher on the last day of term. Even though he was smiling, she could see Mr Peel felt sad as well.

Sad feelings can be painful, and some hurt so much they're hard to bear.

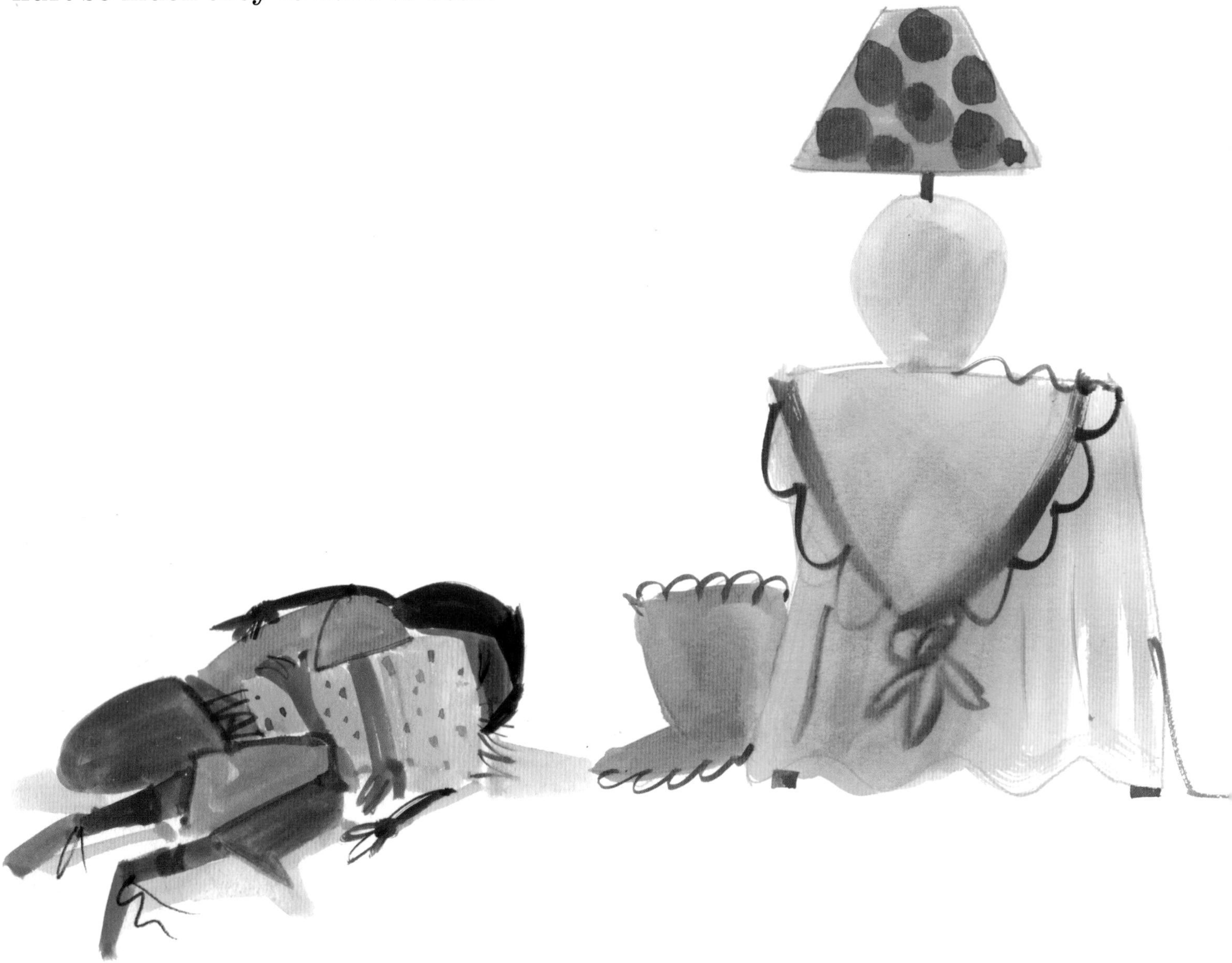

That's how Kate's friend Maddy felt when her parents said they couldn't live together any more.

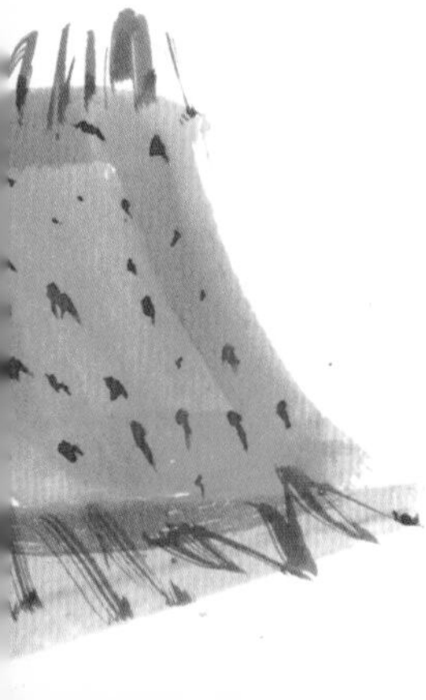

She needed people close to her to understand
how **hurt** she was and to love her even
when she pushed them away.

People who are sad don't always cry.

Crying doesn't always mean
people feel sad, either.

Some people (mostly grown-ups)
cry when they're happy!

Mum cried when
she saw Kate
dancing on stage.

Sam cries when he's
had a bad fall,
or he can't explain
something,
or he's tired.

Kate cries when she
can't think what
she feels, or she's
downright cross.

Feeling **angry** is like feeling *very* cross.

When she saw children playing with fireworks,
Mum felt angry because she knew
how dangerous it was.

She went straight out to tell them to stop – then as soon
as they did, she wasn't angry any more.

Some angry feelings pass quickly, but others run out of control.

Kate was angry with Sam when he threw her dinosaurs out of the window.

(Three of them have never been found.)

She ran into Sam's bedroom, snatched his tank and threw it

down

the

stairs.

Now Sam felt angry.

He slammed the door and kicked the bed, which hurt his foot, which made him even angrier.

Dad shouted when he heard the door bang.

Kate shouted too, but no one could understand what she was saying because she was so angry.

They felt **upset**, and it took Mum a long time to calm them down.

Feeling **jealous** is another way of feeling upset.

Dad says he thinks Fuzzy feels jealous when other dogs come to the house, especially if Mum pays them too much attention.

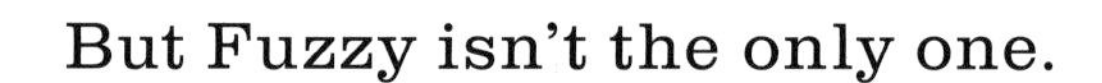

But Fuzzy isn't the only one.

For a while, Sam's friend Pete felt jealous of Sam.

It began when Pete came to stay for the night.

The next day, at school, he teased
Sam for sleeping with a teddy bear.
He persuaded other children to tease him too.

Sam felt hurt, as if he'd been punched right under the ribs.

Pete was bullying Sam because he felt jealous.

He wished *he* had a father who spent time with him, the way Sam's did.
That wishing made Pete feel small and hurt and he couldn't bear it.
So he tried to make Sam feel small and hurt instead,
to make the feeling go away.

Sam talked to his teacher,
who talked to Pete,
who talked to Sam,
who talked to Pete...
and at last they made
friends again.

Sam understood about feeling jealous. Years ago, when Kate was born, he'd felt that way himself.

It was a squirmy, scribbly feeling right in his middle.

Isn't she adorable!

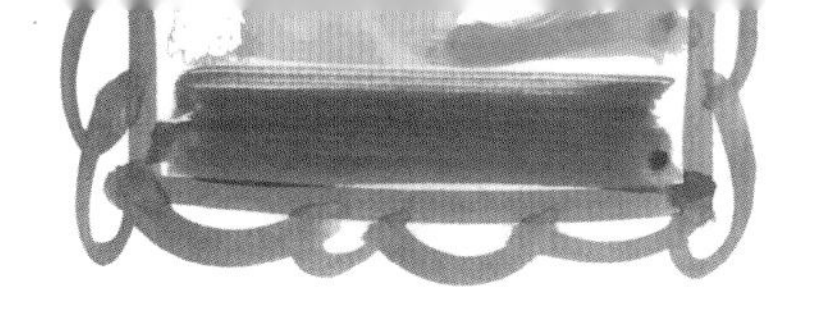

Lots of people came to see the new baby.
They brought presents for her and said how sweet she was, even though she was crumpled and cross and never stopped crying.

Mum and Dad gave Sam a present. It was a shiny fire engine, but it didn't stop the squirmy feeling.

Mum seemed to be caring for little Kate all the time.

Sam didn't like it. It wasn't exactly that he wanted to be a baby again. Or maybe he did in a way. He wasn't sure. But he certainly didn't want Kate to be Mum's baby instead of him.

Also, he couldn't understand why she wanted another child in the first place.

How could she?

He told Dad he would like the baby sent back where she came from. Dad smiled. He said that wasn't possible, but things would get better. Sam was not so sure.

Luckily Dad was right – or right enough. Sometimes Dad looked after Kate, while Sam had Mum to himself.

Don't you want to help, Sam?

He couldn't always enjoy it, though, because he felt too upset.

Other times he got to play with Dad.

Fuzzy felt jealous of Kate as well, so he and Sam became especially close.

As the years passed,
Sam came to see that Kate
wasn't all bad.

She laughed at his jokes and
she was always pleased to see him.

These days Sam and Kate are quite good friends – most of the time...

but not always.

The quarrels come and go. They don't last because,
mostly and overall, there's enough love in the family to go round.

Enough time,

enough listening, enough love.

Author's Note

Every family is different.

My hope, even so, is that reading about the family in this book will offer *all* children a safe way to think about the feelings they, and other people, have.

Here are a few of the questions that might come up: Do I recognize a feeling as it is described in the book or is it different for me? Do I feel it in my body? What is it like? How do I manage difficult feelings? Are there ways I know that help? What other feelings do I have?

Some children might want to talk about their feelings when they read this book with you. Others might prefer to talk about the characters' feelings – or to think without talking, at least for now.

Amanda McCardie has studied infant observation and child development at the Tavistock and Portman NHS Trust, and has also worked as a children's book editor, nursery assistant and teacher. She is the author of two books for children: *The Frog Ballet* and *Davy and Snake*.

Salvatore Rubbino studied illustration at the Royal College of Art in London. His first book for children, *A Walk in New York*, was inspired by a series of paintings he made of Manhattan (shortlisted for the V&A Museum Illustration Awards). He has since published *A Walk in London*, which won an SLA Information Book Award in 2012, and *A Walk in Paris*. He is also the illustrator of *Just Ducks* by Nicola Davies, which was shortlisted for the Kate Greenaway Medal.

Index

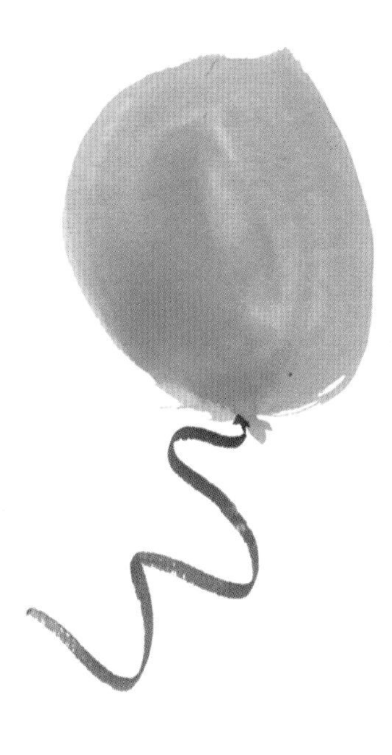

Other books illustrated by Salvatore Rubbino:

A Walk in New York

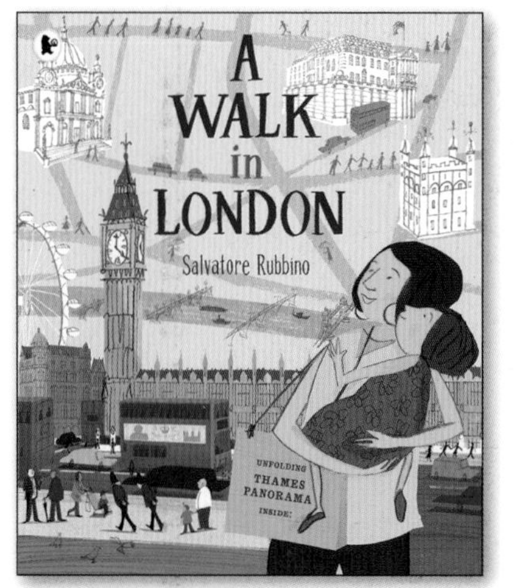

A Walk in London

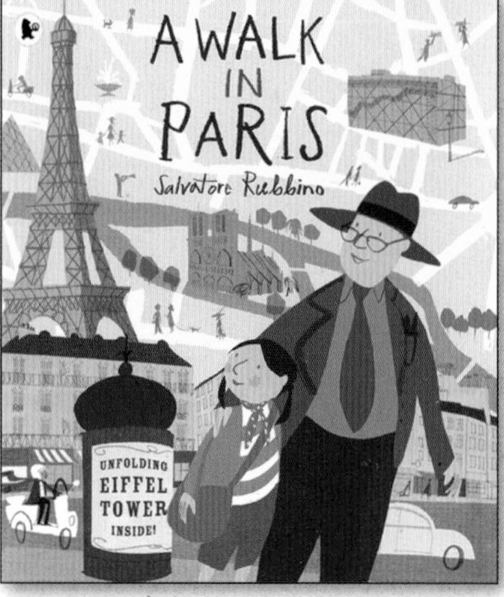

A Walk in Paris

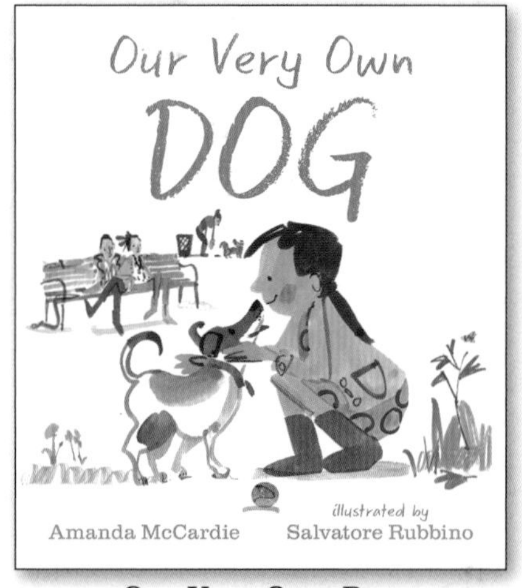

Our Very Own Dog

Just Ducks!

Available from all good booksellers

www.walker.co.uk